GOODBYE AUTUMN, HELLO WINTER

KENARD PAK

GODWINBOOKS

Henry Holt and Company
New York

Hello, late autumn afternoon.

Hello, leaves.

Hello. Now that the wispy winds have come, we fall from the oak tree branches and are swept into the sky!

Hello, robins and cardinals.

Hello! We're ready to fly far, far south.

Hello, horse and sheep. Hello, deer.

Hello! Soon it will be cold,
and we'll stay inside our stables.

We're eating the last of the leaves and berries.
Our fur is becoming thicker for the coming winter.

Hello, chrysanthemums and daisies.

Hello! Even though it's colder, the sunlight warms our leaves and petals.

We'll stay a little longer, until winter comes.

Hello, setting sun.

Hello. The evenings are longer, and the shadows reach farther across the streets.

Hello, clouds.

Hello. We cover the sky like a downy, soft blanket.

Hello, North Star.

Hello! Peeking between clouds,
I shine on the darkest nights.

Hello, evergreens.

Hello. Our pine-needle branches shiver in the wind while you sleep.

Shhh . . . I quiet the juniper and maple trees.

Hello, frost and icicles.

Hello! We decorate
the windows and hang
from the eaves.

Hello, snowflakes.

Hello. We fall in a white, misty curtain and muffle all the sounds around you.

Goodbye, autumn. . . .

Hello, winter!

To Sally,
who guided me forward

Henry Holt and Company
Publishers since 1866
175 Fifth Avenue
New York, New York 10010
mackids.com

Library of Congress Cataloging-in-Publication Data is available.
ISBN 978-1-62779-416-9

Our books may be purchased in bulk for promotional, educational, or business use. Please contact your local bookseller or the
Macmillan Corporate and Premium Sales Department at (800) 221-7945 ext. 5442 or by e-mail at MacmillanSpecialMarkets@macmillan.com.

First Edition—2017 / Designed by Kenard Pak and April Ward
The artist used watercolor and pencil, digitally enhanced, to create the illustrations for this book.
Printed in China by RR Donnelley Asia Printing Solutions Ltd., Dongguan City, Guangdong Province
1 3 5 7 9 10 8 6 4 2